S IN YOUR NIGHTSHIRT

Eerie stories to read in bed

Cover illustration
Scot Jamieson

Interior illustrations
Kathy R. Kaulbach

NIMBUS PUBLISHING LIMITED

© 1987, Children's Writers' Workshop

Sixth printing, June 1994

Text © Children's Writers' Workshop 1986

Illustrations © Kathy R. Kaulbach 1986

Cover illustration © Scot Jamieson 1986

Published by:
Nimbus Publishing Limited
P.O. Box 9301, Station A,
Halifax, N.S. B3K 5N5

Printed and bound in Canada by:
Best Gagné Book Manufacturers
Louiseville, Québec

ISBN 0-920852-94-7

Previously published by the Children's Writers' Workshop
under ISBN 0 969 2342 1 X

Contents

Maestro Warlock, Wizard's Key

Lynn Davies

March 14

Dear Diary:

I don't dare tell Mum or Dad or Cindy or Paul. Who would believe me? They'd think I was spending too much time by myself or watching too much T.V. Only Chaucer knows.

But I tell you everything, dear diary, and here's what happened. As sure as my name is Lydia Kathleen MacGregor, every word I write is absolutely true.

Last night I was alone in the basement playing Asteroids on the computer. The middle of March, snow still on the ground, and we were having a thunder and lightning storm! I felt safer down there, with Chaucer curled up and snoring at my feet. I was punching the keys and watching the screen when suddenly the lights went out and the screen went blank. No electricity.

Mum yelled down not to worry and to find the flashlight in the lower right hand drawer. But before I had a chance to look, the computer screen began to glow pale blue and orange, like the sky at twilight. I heard another distant roll of thunder, the colours wavered, then deepened, and sentences written in strange curly letters appeared on the screen.

What I know can't be explained
What I know can't be contained
If you dare, call on me
Maestro warlock, wizard's key.

"'Maestro warlock, wizard's key'--what's that?" I asked Chaucer.

We didn't have to wait long. First a puff of smoke, then a flash of blue light, followed by a roll of drums, and suddenly a little man wearing a bowler hat and pin-stripe suit appeared, sitting on top of the computer. He coughed, straightened his tie, and twiddled his moustache as he looked around. I was so stunned, I couldn't say a word.

"Ferdinand, the wizard, at your service," he said, bowing low.

"S-Since when do wizards carry briefcases and wear suits," I sputtered.

"Wizards can wear anything they want. In

fact, costumes are one of my specialties," said Ferdinand. "Is this better?"

In a flash he reappeared in a long purple robe embroidered with gold stars, silver comets, and red moons. He wore a tall pointed hat and skinny shoes with bells on the toes.

This was too much for Chaucer. He pounced on the bells with a yelp and a growl. Ferdinand immediately offered Chaucer the meatiest beef bone that little dog had ever seen.

I could see Chaucer was impressed but I needed more convincing.

"How about a piece of chocolate-raspberry cheesecake?" I asked.

Two pieces later, I felt more friendly. When he replaced my old frayed sneaker laces with striped red and blue ones that glowed in the dark, I knew I was on to something good.

Dear Diary: March 15

It's true. Whenever I want Ferdinand, I whisper, "Maestro warlock, wizard's key," and he appears instantly, minus the smoke and drumrolls.

His costumes are great. Today he came as a trapeze artist. He also put out the garbage. Then he washed and dried and the dinner dishes. Luckily no one was home. The dishes flew through the air, fell into the sink, tumbled around on their own, and stacked themselves on the

drainer. Ferdinand used too many suds and broke the butter dish but he made up for that by fixing the dishwasher.

"Just one of those things," I explained, as I stacked cups in the tray this morning. "One good kick and the old thing started up again."

"Where'd you kick it?" asked Mum.

"Right down there, on the side, near the front."

"I don't see how that would work."

"Luck, I guess. You don't need a repairman now. It's fixed."

Was she impressed or puzzled? I'll have to be careful. But I've been thinking of all the presents I can give people. Mum wants a new table lamp for her birthday. Dad wants a canoe, Cindy is always talking about horses, and Paul . . . well, he'd probably like his own spaceship. I can arrange all that, but how would I explain it?

Dear Diary: March 16

A great day. Ferdinand frizzed my hair and finished my math homework before school. Everyone wanted some of my Hawaiian pizza and peanutbutter popcorn at lunch time. After school he helped Chaucer tree the cat next door, peeled the potatoes, and set the table before anyone got home. After dinner he tidied my room, even under the bed, and cleaned my fishtank. By mistake he replaced my four swordtails with a pair of angelfish, but I like them better anyway.

Dear Diary: March 17
        Another great day.
        When Mark Belansky yelled "tin-grin" at me, I muttered, "Ferdinand, do something." Mark's jacket got caught in a door and his ice-cream sandwich landed on the overdue books he was trying to sneak back to the library.

Dear Diary: March 18
        I don't need another day like this one.
        This afternoon the dentist tightened my braces. My mouth hurt. I could only eat soup and I went to bed early.
        "Can't you do something about these braces?" I grumbled. Ferdinand was sitting at the bottom of my bed dressed in a safari suit. "I'm sick of wearing them and I've got another year to go."
        Ferdinand closed his eyes and waved his fingers in the air. Immediately I felt a pressure lift off my teeth. I ran to the mirror, smiled, and for the first time in months saw my teeth. No one could call me "radio transmitter" now.
        Suddenly Chaucer whimpered, moaned, and rolled on the floor. He sneezed, gagged, and ran around the room. He stopped, fell on the floor, and pushed his nose into his paws. He opened his mouth to howl and I saw a gleam of

metal in his mouth.

"Ferdinand!" I shouted. "Chaucer's wearing my braces!"

"Mercy me!" he gasped. "What went wrong. Now let me see . . . " He wrinkled his forehead and closed his eyes to concentrate.

Poor Chaucer was crying and foaming at the mouth.

"Hurry up, stupid," I hissed.

"Oh, Lydia!" he cried in a hurt tone. "What do you expect with a new spell? One little mistake and you get upset. Now let me think."

"Well think fast. I hear my mother."

Sure enough, we heard her walking down the hall calling out something about too much noise and shouldn't I be in bed.

Ferdinand mumbled.

Nothing happened.

He mumbled some more. Chaucer yelped, Ferdinand disappeared, and I suddenly felt that familiar pressure on my teeth just as my mother opened the door.

"Chaucer was chewing on my blue leg warmers," I said weakly as I climbed back into bed.

Dear Diary: March 19

I'm so excited. Tonight I'm on my way to Cuba for some sun.

All day Ferdinand tried to make up for the

braces with promises of cheesecake, no homework for a week, a clean bedroom for a month, and Mark Belansky locked in the school washroom. I finally relented when he suggested a quick trip to a beach with a new bathing suit and all the cherry coke I could drink.

"Can you really do that?" I asked. I was standing in a slush puddle, looking at the dirty snow still lingering under trees and bushes.

"Certainly. It's easy. Bodily travel through space between land masses. I travel that way all the time."

It's 11:00. Mum and Dad are going to bed. We have to wait until everyone is asleep.

Dear Diary: March 20

It was ghastly, what happened. If I die and the world reads this, no one will believe what I'm going to write. But I swear it's true, every bit of it.

Ferdinand, Chaucer, and I were ready to go at 11:30. We sat on the bed, closed our eyes, and Ferdinand muttered something about strange faces, the sea, and the sun. Suddenly I felt light and airy, the wind whistled in my ears, and my legs stretched out behind me. It only seemed like minutes before we were descending and I felt strangely cold.

I landed with a thud on my stomach and opened my eyes. Instead of a sandy beach, I was lying in an empty field with a full orange moon rising in a dark sky. I stood up and looked around. There were no trees or houselights. I couldn't see Chaucer or Ferdinand anywhere.

Something small and black swooped in front of my face. I jumped back, stifling a scream. Bats! Hairy bats! They were everywhere, diving through the air, and my stomach began to churn.

"Get a hold of yourself, Lydia!" I said firmly. "Vampire bats live in South America, these ones won't hurt you. You'd better find Chaucer and Ferdinand."

In the still night I thought I heard voices. I started walking but it was slow going. The ground was soft, like a giant sponge, and I kept sinking into wet cold patches. Shivering, I started climbing a nearby hill. The higher I climbed, the more voices I heard and soon I saw a strange flickering light.

"Firelight," I thought. "Must be a barbecue. Or a bunch of girl guides. Chaucer's probably there already, eating hamburger buns and marshmallows."

But the closer I walked, the more nervous I got. It was the strangest barbecue I'd ever seen. Tall figures in long black robes stood around a cauldron that steamed over a roaring fire.

"A costume party?" I thought doubtfully.

It was too creepy for me. I stepped backwards and fell into a wet hollow.

"Lydia! Is that you?" whispered a voice in

the darkness. I felt a familiar wet nose snuffle my cheek.

"Ferdinand! Where are we?" I hissed, hugging Chaucer with relief.

He cleared his throat nervously. "Northern Scotland in the year 1590. We travelled through time as well as space. I'm afraid I've landed us in a coven of witches. Stay low, I don't want them to see us."

But it was too late. One of them must have spotted me before I fell. Rough hands grabbed our ankles and dragged us into the firelight.

It was a horrible gathering. More witches flew in on pitchforks, shovels, and goats. All of them were dressed in black and were so ugly, with warts and wrinkles and runny noses, that I felt sick to my stomach. But the worst was the pot. Tiny skulls bubbled in a thick red liquid and bits of black fur stuck to the rim. I wished I was at home sitting at the kitchen table, eating a bowl of Cheerios, cleaning my room, even sitting in the dentist's chair. Anything but this.

"What shall we do with them?" shouted one hag with greasy hair.

"I like the girl. We couldn't find any babies tonight. Let's use her!" shrieked another.

"Throw her in!" screeched a third as she came closer.

"Ferdinand! Do something!" I yelled.

"We need her hair and fingernails first,"

cackled another.

"And the dog. We need his ears." They were tying up Chaucer. Ferdinand muttered frantically, disappeared, and reappeared in a hockey uniform. No one noticed. They were all coming towards me.

"Let's pickle her eyes. I need some to mix with my bats' tongues."

"They can wait. It's her heart we need. Throw her in, head first."

Someone tore off my jacket, sharp fingernails dug into my arms, and the last thing I saw was Ferdinand dressed like an Arab waving his hands in the air. They put a black cloth over my head, took off my shoes, and picked me up, chanting something about black-cat bones and tombstone chips. I heard Chaucer yelping. I kicked, screamed, and managed to bite a bony arm through the cloth over my head. But I felt the heat of the fire and heard the pot's hissing as they hauled me closer, chanting:

> Grovelling gophers, babies' blood
> Bits of beetles, clumps of mud
> Boil them hard and find the pieces
> Add some dung and then some leeches.

I began to cry. I thought of Mum and Dad and Cindy and Paul. Then those loathsome things went into their second verse.

> No one stops us, no one dares
> If . . .

11

Suddenly I felt light and airy, the wind whistled in my ears, my legs stretched out behind me, and I tumbled into bed with a piece of black cloth still in my mouth. Chaucer fell on top of me, still tied up. Just in time.

Dear Diary: March 21

Ferdinand sulked when I told him he had to go.

"This won't look good on my resume," he said. "After a 250 year apprenticeship, you're my first assignment. Give me another chance, Lydia?"

"No way," I said. "Chaucer nearly lost his ears and I almost became witch's soup because of your bumbling."

"At least write me a good reference," he pleaded.

"You've got to be kidding," I snapped. "After what happened last night?"

But he looked so upset I finally wrote that he was never late for an appointment and knew how to dress for any occasion. After all, he had done me a lot of favors this week and his outfits were impressive. The last time I saw him he was wearing steel armour, with the visor down, and carrying a shield and double-edged sword. A long red feather hung from the helmet. He was also seated on a white horse right in the middle of my bedroom. Quite breathtaking, but I was afraid the horse might leave something on my carpet. I also wanted to see the last of him, so I wished him luck, waved good-bye, and ran downstairs.

The dishwasher broke down again, Mum kicked it, and hurt her foot. But I don't mind washing dishes anymore. I'm lucky I still have my hair and all my fingernails. I'm lucky I still have a dog. And next time there's a thunder and lightning storm, I'm turning the computer off and going to bed.

It's Your Turn

Kathy Densmore

"Sleeping bag, one bag of Oreo cookies, three Masters of the Universe comics." Jeff stood, blond hair blowing in the warm summer breeze, checking each item with his list. He crammed his overstuffed knapsack to capacity.

"Are you sure we won't be cold?" asked Tom, standing beside him doing the same.

"Heck, no. It's July. Whoever heard of anyone getting cold in July? Besides, we're going to light a fire, remember? Oh, that reminds me, matches."

"I've got them, said Tom, holding up the book of matches his mom had given him before leaving with a firm warning to be careful.

"That's it. Let's go," said Jeff, heading

toward the shore. "We don't have a lot of daylight hours left," he remarked, glancing at the horizon. Tom followed reluctantly. It wasn't that he didn't want to go. It was just that he had heard stories about Clam Island--stories about ghosts and treasures. When he mentioned these stories Jeff had just laughed at him.

"You sound like my grandpa Ned," he had said.

"Oh, maybe he's right," Tom thought as he climbed into the boat and prepared to shove off. "After all, what could happen in one night?"

* * * * * * * * * * * *

Ned Gunther slowly made his way through the path which led to his grandson's house. His eighty-five years were evident now as he stepped carefully for fear of falling. His hair, once golden, was now white and his strong and agile body was frail and bent. The only remaining aspect of his youth was his spirit. With dancing eyes he would sit and tell stories of his younger days as a fisherman and the fun he had along the bay. Ned thought of Jeff as he walked, so much like himself, so full of vim and vigor. Yes, there was a special place in his heart for the boy, he had to admit that, as he reached the back door of his son's house, knocked and entered the kitchen.

Jeff's father, having his evening cup of

15

coffee at the kitchen table, glanced up when he heard the door opening. "Evening, Dad. How's the arthritis tonight?"

"Oh, not bad," Ned answered, finding a chair beside his son. "Knees are a little stiff, but everything else works. Where's Jeff?" Ned asked, surprised at the silence in the house.

"He and Tom Winters went to spend the night out on Clam Island." Ken filled his pipe then settled back in his chair to enjoy his father's visit.

"What? You let them go by themselves?" Ned asked, leaning forward to face his son.

"Dad, you know Jeff can take care of himself and Tom is a good kid. I know his father."

"Ken, for Heaven's sake, boy, what about the ghost?"

"Dad, what are you talking about?"

"I'm talking about the ghost!"

"Which ghost story are you talking about now?"

Nervously, Ned began to tell the legend that was as much a part of his youth as fishing boats and the bay. "Years ago, so they say, boats carried lumber from Hubbards down to Barbados. There they traded the lumber for sugar and material and things like that.

"Well, one time a crew was given gold coins for payment instead of the usual things. On the way back home five of the crew members stole

16

the gold coins and left the boat. They decided to bury their treasure on Clam Island for safekeeping.

"While they were on the island, an argument began between two of the crew members. They couldn't decide how to divide the treasure. The argument turned into a bloody fight and it ended with one of the men cutting the throat of the other.

"Well, the other men didn't really know what to do with the body, so they decided to bury it with the treasure. They threw the body face down on top of the chest and quickly covered in the hole.

"They say the ghost of the dead man guards the treasure until one hundred years are up. Then he can free himself and will walk the island looking for someone to replace him." Ned glanced at his son, who was busily refilling his pipe.

"Well, yes, the ghost--what of it?" Ken asked impatiently.

"I've been told that if the ghost can lure you to the treasure, you will become the next victim and the ghost is freed."

"Oh, Dad, for Pete's sake! I suppose you're going to tell me that this is the hundredth year!"

"Yes, man, according to the legend, it is. This is the year!"

"Listen, Dad, I want you to stop this

nonsense. You'll only get yourself upset for no reason."

"By gum, I'm tellin' ya, those boys are in danger!" Ned yelled, jumping up from his chair and heading toward the window. "Oh no!"

"Dad, what's wrong now?"

"I knew it. I just knew it!"

"Dad, what are you talking about?"

"It is said that when the moon is high in the sky and shines a silvery path to the shore, the ghost will roam the island. People say he can be seen standing on the edge of the island beckoning people to come. Ken, look at the moon!"

"Dad, don't!"

"I've got to go!"

"Dad, you can't go out there by yourself."

"I gotta go. It may be too late."

"OK, I'll come with you."

"Grab a mirror."

"What?"

"Grab a mirror, I said."

"Why?"

"Never mind, just do it!"

Ken obeyed, grabbing the hand mirror from the bathroom shelf. He was out the door just in time to see his father reach the shore, waving his hands wildly and pointing to the bright moon and the silvery shadow across the water.

18

*   *   *   *   *   *   *   *   *   *   *   *

"I thought you said you knew how to light a fire," said Tom, rubbing his hands furiously.

"I do." Jeff fumbled with the limp cardboard in his hand. "But the matches are wet. Remember, you dropped them getting out of the boat."

"Oh, yeah," Tom answered sheepishly.

"Can I help?" Startled, the boys turned to see a very tall, thin man standing behind them.

"Who . . . who . . . are you?" Jeff asked, losing some of his self- assurance.

"Elijah's the name," the stranger replied. "Having trouble with your fire, are ya? Here, let me help." Squatting down in front of the fire, he began rearranging the birchbark and twigs the boys had piled in the center of their campfire.

"We don't have any matches , you know," Jeff piped up.

"Oh, we don't need matches." When he was finished, Elijah reached into a leather pouch, attached to his belt buckle, and took out what appeared to be a small flat stone. He struck it hard against a rock and immediately a spark ignited. Gently, Elijah placed the rock underneath the pile of sticks and branches.

Jeff sat back and silently studied this old man as he gently coaxed the burning flame. He seems nice enough, Jeff thought. But there was something about this man that made him uneasy. Jeff wondered if it was the way he was dressed or the way he talked. He didn't know, but something wasn't quite right.

"Jeff, listen to this," Tom was saying excitedly.

"What?" Jeff asked, pulling himself back to reality.

"Listen to what Elijah is saying."

"Yes, there were lots of pirates and treasures around these parts in the late I800's. In fact, there's a treasure buried right here on this island. What do you think of that, me boys?"

"There is?" Tom asked, "Where?"

"Over there." He motioned to the opposite side of the island.

"Can you take us to it?" Tom asked.

"Sure, me boy!"

"I don't know," Jeff responded nervously, feeling out of control of the situation. Jeff looked at Tom for support. But Tom seemed perfectly at ease with this stranger.

Why don't I trust him? Jeff thought to himself. What is it that seems so . . . .

"Ah, it's already dark, you know," Jeff added.

"Oh, there's plenty of light. Moon's bright," Elijah responded with ease. "Good night for digging. Don't worry 'bout the shovel. I've got two of 'em."

"You mean we're really gonna dig for treasure?" Tom asked excitedly.

"Yeah, I've been digging all day and I'm 'bout there. That's why I came to ya. Heard you talking and thought you could help me finish. It's hard to do it by m'self, you know."

"Well , let's go then," Tom yelled, looking at Jeff for approval.

"Well . . . yeah, OK," Jeff answered. This is ridiculous, he thought. I'm getting as superstitious as Grandpa.

"Great!" Tom yelled, jumping up, looking for his jacket.

Elijah turned, concealing a satisfied smile as they quickly cleaned up around the campfire and prepared to leave.

"This is great!" Tom commented enthusiastically as they followed Elijah through the wooded path. Jeff, pulling back, beckoned Tom to do the same.

"Tom," he whispered, " do you trust this guy?"

"Yeah, sure, don't you?"

"I don't know. There's something about him that gives me the creeps."

"C'mon Jeff. He's a nice guy."

"I can't help it. He gives me the creeps."

"Look, if he really bothers you, we'll just go and see the treasure pit and then we'll leave. OK?"

"OK," Jeff answered, still not sure what was in store.

"You there , me boys?" Elijah yelled from some distance ahead.

"Yeah, we're coming," Jeff answered, glancing sideways at Tom who suddenly looked a little less enthusiastic. "Come on, let's go," Jeff whispered tugging at Tom's sleeve and heading in the direction of Elijah's voice.

* * * * * * * * * * * *

"Hurry, Ken, hurry," Ned yelled as Ken labouriously rowed toward the island.

"Dad, what do you plan to do once you get there?" Ken asked, puffing.

Ned looked at Ken intently. "Ken, I've never told you this before and, in fact, I thought I would never have to. I thought it was a secret I would take to my grave. But I see the time has come."

"Dad, what do you mean?" Ken sat and stared as his father told the family secret.

"You see, your great grandfather was a pirate. In fact, he was one of the five pirates who stole the gold coins."

"Great Grandfather Murray?" Ken asked.

"No, your Great Grandfather Ned--the one I was named after! So our great grandfather killed this pirate. Well, he didn't actually kill the man, but he was there when the killing happened. He carried the burden with him all his life and swore me to secrecy. I'm asking you to do the same."

"Yeah, OK," Ken replied, not quite believing what he was hearing. "But what about the mirror?"

"They say that the ghost is ashamed of his deeds and can't bear to see his own reflection."

"Oh, I see. So, you plan to trick this so-called ghost ito facing himself, sort of speaking."

"Well, we'll see," Ned answered as they reached the island. "Here we are. I can see the coals of their fire burning from here. Let me go and see if they're about," Ned said, attempting to stand in the boat.

"Look out, Dad," Ken yelled as the boat dangerously tipped to one side. "I'll go. You stay here."

Ken left, leaving Ned fidgeting.

"They're not here," Ken yelled, running toward the boat. "Their gear is there, but they're not around."

"OK, help me out! I've got to get my bearings." Ken helped his father out and watched as he paced back and forth mumbling to himself.

"We need to go to the north side of the island," Ned said, returning.

Quickly they stepped back into the boat and shoved off in the direction of the north side.

"We're almost there," Elijah said as they plodded through a densely wooded area. "Just over here through these bushes," Elijah said, entering a clearing, "behind them trees."

The boys followed silently. Jeff, sensing Elijah's anxiety, watched carefully as he went directly to a large hole beside a tree.

"OK, me boys! This is it!" Elijah grabbed one of the two shovels standing against a nearby tree. He jumped into the pit and began to dig. Tom and Jeff stood above, watching intently, not quite sure what to do. After a short while, Elijah climbed out of the pit and handed the shovel to Tom.

"How about you guys digging for a while? It's hard work, you know."

"OK," Tom answered, intent on finding the treasure. Jeff found the other shovel and joined Tom in the pit. Both boys set to work. The ground was soft so the digging was easy. As Jeff worked, he tried to figure out what was so familiar about this man. Suddenly he knew. His grandfather. He had told him about a treasure and something about a pirate ghost. What did he say about the ghost? Oh, I wish I had listened to my grandpa, Jeff fretted to himself. Wait a minute . . . Pirate, knickers, baggy shirt . . . high boots. Jeff stopped

digging and looked up at Elijah standing at the edge of the pit. Coal black eyes stared back.

"You're . . . you're the ghost," Jeff stammered, backing away from Elijah.

"That's right, m'boy!" Elijah cackled gleefully. "And now it's your turn," he yelled, pointing a finger at the two boys below him. Squatting, he picked up a handful of dirt and began throwing it in the pit. Frightened and trembling, the boys huddled together in a corner listening to the evil Elijah above them.

"I've done my time!" he continued. "One hundred years and now I'm free!" Faster and faster he threw the dirt. First with one hand and then with both. "You're trapped! There ain't nothing you can do!"

"But *I* can."

Elijah's head jerked in the direction of the voice. Startled, he stepped backward when he recognized the old man standing a short distance away. "Ned," Elijah was saying. "Is that you?"

"Yes, it's me, Elijah. What are you doing with these boys?"

"I've done my time! It's their turn!"

"No, Elijah. You belong with the treasure. It's your treasure. You wanted it all. Now you have it!" Ned answered, moving slowly toward Elijah, his eyes never leaving his face. Quickly, Ken rushed toward the boys. He helped them out of the pit, then backed them out of the way.

"We've got to help Grandpa," Jeff whispered to his father.

"Sh . . . sh," Ken answered, watching his father so intent in conversation with this ghost.

Slowly Ned withdrew the mirror from his jacket pocket, and catching the light of the moon, shone it directly into Elijah's face. "Here, look at yourself."

"No, don't!"

"You're a thief, look!" Ned yelled, holding the mirror to his face. "You belong down below. Where it's dark."

"Noooooo," he yelled, bringing both arms up to shield his face from the light. "Nooooo," he repeated. Elijah began to tremble and shake uncontrollably. His whole body seemed to collapse.

"Go. Now!" Ned yelled.

Suddenly he was gone!

"Grandpa," Jeff yelled, "are you OK?"

"Yes, my boy, I'm fine! How are you?"

"We're OK. Grandpa, the ghost knew your name. How? How did you know where we were?"

"Wait a minute,"Ken said, moving toward his father. "I think we'd better get your grandpa home. He's had a long day."

"I'll tell you about it in the boats, boys, but first I want you to help me fill int he pit."

"But, Dad," Ken protested.

"It's best, my son. The treaure is cursed.

There was blood shed when it was buried and there must be blood shed to claim it. It would only bring trouble to our family. I want no part of it."

Shortly after, the pit was once again filled in and they were heading for home.

Now, deep, deep in the ground on an isolated island, a man lies face down on top of an ancient chest. Clawing and scraping the ground around him, he plans his revenge and waits for the next hundred years to pass.

The Three Aunties

Felicity Finn

I wasn't afraid of the aunties at first. It was only later, after we'd seated them on the living room couch in front of the TV, just as if they were watching a show, that a little shiver of fear went down my back. They looked so real.

The aunties were my mother's idea. Ever since she'd got her new job as set-designer at the theatre, she'd been planning a big celebration, and wanted something unusual to make it a party her friends would remember.

It took us almost three weeks to make them. First my mother collected everything we needed from thrift and antique shops, fabric stores and costume places, and then we started work.

"You can be in charge of limbs and bodies, Jeremy," my mother said. "I'll take care of the tricky bits, like the faces and fingers."

The legs were the easiest. I just stuffed three pairs of pantyhose full of cotton batting and stuck the feet into shoes. The faces were made of stuffed nylon stocking too. My mother had a lot of fun putting the expressions on. First she stitched a nose, ears, a lip line and eyelids. Then she sewed in wrinkles, dimples, crowsfeet, and creases by the cheeks and mouth. By the time she'd added makeup, wigs and clothes, the three aunties looked almost alive.

"We must name them, Jeremy," my mother said. "To me they look *exactly* like a Mabel, a Gladys and a Dotty. What do you think?"

"Sure."

"I fear old Mabel is a bit of a prude," my mother said, looking the first doll over with satisfaction.

"I think we made Gladys too fat," I commented.

My mother sighed. "Yes, she really should try to lose a few pounds. And that dress! Obviously poor Gladys has absolutely no taste when it comes to clothes. It looks like she bought her entire outfit at a secondhand store." We giggled.

"Now Dotty's what I call a real doll," my mother said. "I'll bet she broke a few hearts in her day."

30

They all looked like real dolls to me, sitting there on the couch. So human, in fact, that I half expected them to speak. A strange shiver ran down my spine.

On the night of the party I pretended to go up to bed, but crept down later and watched everything through the bannisters. The aunties stole the show. All my mother's friends loved them. "Charming! So original! So lifelike!" they exclaimed delightedly. As we'd hoped, some of the guests, when they first entered the room, thought the aunties were real people. I actually saw one of my mother's co-workers pass a tray of smoked sausages to Gladys, then blush, and look around to see if anyone had noticed. By the end of the evening, a slightly tipsy professor was sitting on the couch with his arm around Dotty, deep in conversation with her. Doctor Suggs was waltzing around the room with Mabel and her cane.

The next morning I was downstairs early, searching the living room for leftover treats. A few cold sausages remained, as well as some potato chips and five chocolates on a tray. I was crouched down feeling around under an armchair for a bowl of chip dip, when suddenly I thought I heard someone clear their throat. I froze. Then a voice quite near me said, "Imagine, going to bed and leaving all this mess and clutter behind. Didn't even wash the dishes! What kind of a

household is this?"

The hairs on my neck bristled up. I scrunched down very small and listened. I heard another, younger voice reply, "But it was a lovely party, I must say. That professor Ricketts is *such* a charming conversationalist. So intellectual!"

"Really," snapped the first voice, "I'm surprised at you, Dotty. Letting yourself be flattered by that nasty red-faced fellow with wine stains on his shirt. He wasn't even wearing a tie. Goodness!"

"Why, Mabel, I declare! I saw you dancing with that handsome doctor and enjoying every minute of it."

"I certainly did not enjoy it, Dotty my dear.

He simply grabbed me and began to waltz. What could I do? I tried my best to kick him in the shins and trip him up with my cane."

"The lady of the house may be a terrible housekeeper," said a third voice, "but she does know how to cook. That food looked good enough to eat. I was afraid all evening that someone would hear my stomach growling."

Slowly, I raised my head over the back of the armchair. As I'd suspected, there was no one else in the room. No one, that is, besides the three aunties, who were sprawled on the couch just as they'd been left the night before. Stuffed dolls cannot speak, I told myself firmly, no matter how real they look. It's impossible. But I felt cold and shivery all the same, and all the ghost stories I'd ever heard popped into my mind. Then I almost laughed out loud. Of course! I thought. My mother, or some of her crazy friends, have rigged this up to entertain me. I began to search under the furniture and behind the cushions for a hidden tape recorder. But there was none to be found, not even under the aunties' couch.

My next thought was, Aha! Speakers hidden in their stuffing! My mother could be speaking into a microphone from her room. It would be just like her. But none of the voices had sounded like hers. I approached the aunties a little timidly. After all, I wasn't used to poking around in old ladies' hair and clothing.

I began with Mabel. She was the oldest of the three, dressed all in black. I looked under her small black hat and veil, and under her grey wig. I checked her cane and the little silver locket around her neck. I squeezed her all over-- under her shawl, under her dress--but there was no hard bump to be found. Her little eyes seemed to be staring at me with disgust. I finished searching her as quickly as I could.

Dotty was next. She was the youngest and the prettiest of the aunties. She wore a navy blue suit and high heeled button shoes. There were feathers on her hat and a fur tossed over one shoulder. I even checked her beaded handbag and her long cigarette holder. There was no trace of a speaker.

That left only Gladys. Her flowered dress was very tight over her chest and her feet bulged over her shoes. She wore a shiny stole, several rings and necklaces, and large pearl earrings. I began squeezing her chubby arms. Suddenly, to my horror, she began to giggle uncontrollably. I drew back my hands in terror. She kept on laughing and hiccupping, and gasped out, "Ooh, I just couldn't help it, I'm so ticklish."

"You're alive!" I gasped, scrambling back out of reach.

"Do I look dead?" Gladys giggled. Mabel's shoulders slumped and Dotty looked offended.

"Now you've done it," Mabel said to Gladys, and turning to me, she said, "What a dreadful boy you are, going around poking and tickling elderly ladies. Did no one teach you manners?"

I had never in my life felt so shocked and confused and just plain petrified. "Sorry," I stammered, drawing back a few more steps. "I--I thought you were just stuffed dolls."

"Stuffed dolls, indeed!" Mabel sniffed. "You ought to be ashamed of yourself. Now, if you would be so kind, you might help us out of these undignified positions and set us up straight."

I hesitated. I was pretty frightened, but still a little suspicious. Just in case anyone was listening, I said very loudly, "This is a great conversation, whoever you are, but you haven't tricked me, so why not turn off the microphone and we can talk in person." As I was speaking, I heard my mother walk down the hall to the bathroom, and knew she couldn't be behind the voices. In fact, no one had had a chance to 'bug' the aunties at any time since they'd been finished. So they could actually talk all by themselves! Unbelievable! I felt scared, but much too interested to leave. I approached the couch cautiously, and set them up straight, being careful to touch them as little as possible.

"Thank-you," said Mabel primly.

"Young man, what is your name?" asked Dotty.

"J-Jeremy."

"Delightful name. I'm Dotty, and these are my cousins, Mabel and Gladys."

"I know," I whispered, holding out my hand to show I did have some manners. None of them took it. I knew they could move a little, enough to shrug or move their fingers, but I suddenly wondered if they were able to actually walk. I imagined them prowling through the house at night, creeping up the stairs to my room. "Excuse me," I stammered, "but I just wondered, I mean, can you walk?"

"Walk?" Gladys giggled. "He wants to know if we can walk."

"Bum leg," Mabel said with dignity, pointing to her cane.

"Of course we can't," said Dotty. "Could you walk on legs like these?" They exchanged amused glances. "We think of ourselves as purely decorative and--" She broke off as my mother came down the stairs.

"Oh, good morning, Jeremy," my mother said. "The party was a smash! Ah, talking to the aunties, I see. They were the hit of the party. Have you made breakfast?"

I followed her into the kitchen, and while she made tea and cinnamon toast, I tried to find out just what was going on.

"Uh, Mom, uh, you don't believe in ghosts, do you?"

"Certainly I do! All my life I've been dying to meet one. (No pun intended.) Jeremy, you haven't found one, have you?"

"Mom, have you or your friends rigged up the three aunties to talk?"

"No--but what a wonderful idea! Why didn't I think of it for the party? Just imagine the effect!"

Her denial seemed so genuine I knew my worst fears were true.

"Why do you ask, Jeremy?"

"Just joking," I said with a shrug. She went back to her tea, looking disappointed. I knew that if she ever realized exactly what she had created, she'd be so ecstatic that she'd probably go on making life-sized stuffed dolls until the house was filled up. I could just imagine dozens of wrinkled old creatures-- sitting at the table, curled up on the beds, waiting by the phone, soaking in the tub. And all jabbering away at the top of their lungs! The thought was a little frightening. Pretty horrible, as a matter of fact. Three of them were quite enough for me.

By the end of the week it began to look as if the aunties were there to stay. My mother thought them such a charming addition to the house--like pieces of art or furniture--that she simply left them on the couch. I was dying to tell someone about them, but somehow I knew that the presence of three talking dummies on your livingroom couch was a secret that should be kept to yourself; I didn't want to be locked up for the rest of my life.

I spent every spare minute with the aunties. I wasn't sure if they liked me, exactly, but I think I fascinated them as much as they did me. They were interested in everything I told them about school, and the city, and they loved looking out the picture window at the passing traffic and people. They seemed completely ignorant about a lot of things. The TV, stereo, VCR, and even the lights and the telephone and the radiators filled them with amazement. "No fireplace! No woodstove!" they always said, "and it's so warm in here."

I showed them how to work the remote

control, and they watched TV every afternoon when the house was empty. I think they watched the soaps. When I'd get home from school they'd be full of remarks about the shocking behaviour of the actors. But they loved the slang, and began using expressions such as 'Dry up' and 'Get real', and their favourite, 'Get stuffed', which used to make them practically roll on the floor with laughter.

I was really becoming quite fond of the aunties, and had completely lost any fear of them, when one Saturday, as I was searching my mother's closet for my tennis shoes, I came across this little album full of old photographs printed on thin metal squares. I brought it out into the light to see better, and there, on the first page, was a picture of Mabel, Gladys and Dotty, sitting on an old-fashioned sofa in a room I didn't recognize. My fingers shook as I held it closer to check if it was really them. It was. I rushed downstairs and shoved the picture into my mother's hands. "Who--who are they?" I demanded in a shaky voice.

She turned the picture over and pointed to the names engraved on the back. "Mabel, Gladys and Dotty," she read with a grin.

"But," I cried hoarsely, "they were real people once?"

She smiled again. "I found this old book of tintypes in my favourite antique shop. When I saw this picture, I suddenly got the idea for the three aunties. And the names on the back were so perfect, I simply had to call them that. I even tried to find clothes like these. Why are you looking so strange, Jeremy? Are you feverish?"

I rushed from the room, unable to explain my fear. Of course, my mother had no idea that by making the aunties she had resurrected the dead. I locked myself in the bathroom and thought about what I should do. How do you get rid of ghosts in the house? I thought about taking the aunties and throwing them into a closet where I wouldn't have to look at them--or listen to them. But I imagined them bumping against the closet door in the night, trying to get out, and decided that three ghosts in a closet would be much worse than three ghosts on the couch. I thought of giving them away, but I didn't know anyone who'd want them. I even thought of trying to sell them to a costume shop, although I knew my mother would kill me if I did. Then I had the idea of simply throwing them out in the garbage--but I was worried that they'd come back to haunt me. Finally, I actually considered trying to unstuff them--take them apart limb by limb so that they would no longer exist. But I imagined their shrieks and howls if I started pulling them to pieces, and the thought filled me with horror. I knew I could never do it; they were practically my friends. Or had been, until I realized they were real live dead ghosts.

At last I reached the conclusion that I would have to face the aunties sometime and tell them what I knew. Very slowly, I walked downstairs and into the livingroom.

"Good afternoon," they all said politely.

"Listen," I said, as I pulled out their picture, "just who are you and what are you doing here, and why don't you just go back where you came from?"

They were so interested in the picture that for once they didn't even comment on the rudeness of my questions. They passed it back and forth, exclaiming at the wonderful likeness, and the memories it brought back.

"But you were real people once!" I said.

They ignored me. "This was taken just before the fire," Gladys told the others. "I remember smelling smoke as we were talking to the photographer."

"What fire?" I cried, but my voice stayed trapped in my throat. "Don't you see?" I said. "You're dead! All three of you are dead!"

Mabel raised her eyebrows. "So what?" she said.

"But that means you're--you're ghosts!"

"What did you think we were, talking dolls?" Dotty asked with a giggle.

"I don't want to see you anymore," I said. "Go away. Please."

"What are you scared of?" Dotty asked."

"Yes," Gladys added, "what's changed?"

"Nothing, I guess," I said slowly, "but--don't you *mind*, being ghosts, being dead? Isn't it eerie for you?"

"How do we know *you're* not a ghost?" they said.

"Because I'm real," I said, feeling slightly ridiculous. We argued a little bit more, and eventually I began to relax. They were just the same as they'd always been. "But what are we going to do?" I asked.

"Why do anything?" said Mabel. "This is a comfortable couch. We're becoming rather fond of the TV, and--" she coughed in embarrassment.

"What Mabel is trying to say," Gladys explained, "is that we've become rather fond of *you*, Jeremy."

"You're not bad company--for a real person," Dotty said with a wink.

I felt myself getting red with embarrassment. It was their first compliment. "Oh, get stuffed," I joked, and we all had a good laugh.

"There you are!" my mother exclaimed a moment later, poking her head around the corner. "Jeremy, there's someone here I'd like you to meet."

I looked up. My mother slowly walked into the room, her arms around three well-dressed elderly gentlemen. "Surprise!" she said.

I realized with a sudden shock that they were not old gentlemen at all, but three large stuffed-stocking dolls. "Jeremy," my mother said with a wide grin, "I'd like you to meet Edward, Mort and Harvey. They'll be great company for the aunties, don't you think?"

I felt my hands go cold and clammy.

I watched her settle the newcomers into comfortable chairs. "We'll all be one big happy family!" she said. "Well, what do you think of the uncles, Jeremy? Jeremy? Where are you off to? Come back . . . ."

The Possession

K. A. Harnish

"Going for a walk along the rocks, Gran!" Molly yelled as she bounded out the worn screen door. "Be back in awhile!"

Molly's grandmother watched out the kitchen window.

"Thirteen years old and as fearless as they come, that girl," she muttered.

"A tough-minded MacKinnon, that's for sure," piped up Grandpa, taking a sip of his coffee. "Gets her stubborness from your side of the family, Gert," he chuckled, getting up from the table.

Standing at the window, they followed Molly's confident strides as she hiked through the willow grass bordering the rocky ocean shoreline.

Gert and Ted MacKinnon had raised their only grandchild for twelve and a half years, ever since the tragic death of Molly's parents in a car accident.

"Those rocks can be dangerous, the way they roll over each other so loosely," Molly's grandmother worried.

"Oh, now Gert, you always worried about her mother's adventures on the rocks, too. She'll be fine," reassured Grandpa, "just fine."

They could barely see Molly in the distance as she clambered down over the grassy knoll onto the rocks.

* * * * * * * * * * * *

"I should've brought a jacket. The wind's getting cold."

Molly's WHAM T-shirt was not enough to keep her warm when the winds came up offshore.

"Guess Grandpa was right about the ocean breezes changing the weather on a whim."

Molly noticed dark clouds beginning to form as she turned to climb up the rocks and run back for her jacket. Out of the corner of her eye, she caught a glimpse of something hazy swirling out over the water. It looked like a small fog patch hovering a short distance out.

"That's weird, my glasses must need cleaning again," she said, shrugging it off.

Scrambling, using her hands to cling on to the loose rocks, she climbed back to the grassy top. She hoisted herself onto the edge and sat for a moment glancing out to sea. Molly stood up and immediately became aware that the wind was blowing much stronger. With her curly hair whipping her face, she hesitated, and looked out at the ocean once more. Knocked over by a sudden gust, Molly lay on the ground unable to move. Molly was frozen in terror, her heart beating so hard she could hear the pounding in her ears. Something flew into her mind and took over. A dream-like picture appeared. A faceless figure came into view, groping on hands and knees, frantically searching for something. From a distance, a frenzied voice echoed, "Find it, find it, find it!" The images began to swirl faster and faster until it was a complete blur. Then as fast a the wind was sucked back out to sea, so were the images. Soaked in sweat, Molly regained control and lay shivering in the lanky grass. She slowly rose to her feet looking around. Something had possessed her for a moment and vanished. Frightened and confused, Molly found herself running as fast as she could towards the house.

"Gran," Molly shrieked as she burst through the kitchen door, "Something or someone just talked to me from out of nowhere!"

"Molly, my girl, you're out of breath. Sit and calm down a moment."

"But Gran, you're not going to believe this. I was just coming back for my jacket when, BOOM, something flattened me! Honest!"

"Well, maybe you tripped, dear, and hurt your head. Here, let me take a look," Gran said as she moved towards Molly.

"It wants me to find something, but everything was swirling around in my head so fast, I couldn't figure out what it was!"

Molly heard herself try to explain. The look on her grandmother's face told her she was not making any sense.

"Molly, take a glass of water and sit down. You're all flushed," Gran insisted, motioning towards a chair. "Don't you think you've done enough running for today, young lady?"

"But Gran," said Molly, hesitating. She was completely unsure of how to explain what happened. In a daze, she drank her glass of water.

Later that evening in her room, Molly tried to come up with an explanation.

"Maybe it was something totally awesome, like the wind blowing a voice all the way over the ocean from England, or something. Or maybe it didn't happen at all and I just thought I heard a voice . . . couldn't move . . . saw a person . . . . Oh, what's going on here? Maybe I shouldn't tell anyone 'cause they'll just think I'm going out of my mind or something." Exhausted, Molly climbed into bed and rolled over. Pulling her blankets up over her shoulder, her last thoughts were that she would not remember any of this in the morning.

In the weeks that followed, Molly continued to have these 'moments'. Something, like a whirlwind, entered her mind and took over, showing the same scene of a faceless person, bent over, clawing at the ground. The image flashed through her head, then vanished, leaving her dazed. They occurred at the worst times, like at a basketball game with all her friends. Molly found herself still standing after everyone else sat down, finished with their cheer for a point scored. A guy behind her told Molly that her back wasn't nearly as exciting as the game, so could she please sit down. Molly could feel herself turn red with embarrassment.

"What is it you want? Tell me!" Molly blurted out loud. This time, she was in school speaking to the back of her friend's head.

"Tell you what, Molly?" Laura asked as she turned around in her seat.

"Laura Gilbert!" said Mrs. Warner sternly, "Please turn around and do your work. And Molly MacKinnon, please keep your comments to yourself during the test."

It happened again in the school bathroom. Flashes of light and moving pictures whirled inside her head like a buzzing fly wanting to land.

"Please tell me what's going on here," Molly pleaded as she stood shaking in front of the mirror.

"Well, it looks like your hair has frizzed out again, Molly," answered Laura. "Here, you want my brush?"

"What?" Molly asked, surprised at finding Laura beside her.

"I said, 'Do you want my brush?' Gee, Molly, what's with you? You're not making much sense these days. It's like you're somewhere else. What's wrong?"

"Listen Laura, you promise not to laugh?"

"Sure," said Laura, her curiosity piqued.

"Well, I'm sure I'm possessed or something!"

"What? You're kidding aren't you?" questioned Laura.

"I mean it! Something eerie has been happening to me. Something or someone is taking control of me and wants me to find something for it," whispered Molly.

"Get real!" said Laura, "You sure you're not dreaming this, Molly?"

"Look, even though it scares me, I think if I could just figure out what it wants, it'll go away," Molly said hoping her friend didn't think she was too strange.

"Gee, Molly," suggested Laura, patting her on the back, "maybe you should see a doctor or something."

Even her good friend Laura thought she was nuts! Molly decided she was the only one who could do something about this.

Returning to the grassy knoll overlooking the ocean, where the first possession occurred, Molly perched on the edge of the rocks. Heart pounding down to her hiking boots, she knew she had to confront this thing head on. Molly spoke into the wind billowing around her.

"Look, whatever you are, we gotta get something straight. You're scaring me to death. I know you're trying to tell me something, but I just don't understand it. Slow down, so I can figure out what you want with me!"

The minutes seemed to drag.

"Come on, wind, bring on whatever it is that's making me crazy," she shouted a little fearfully.

Just when she was about to give up, she felt a gentle breeze swirl and encircle her. Her heart beat faster as the pit of her stomach churned with fear. She waited for the possession to occur. But something was different this time. A young girl appeared on her hands and knees, head bent, searching for something on the rocks below. Frantically, she overturned the smaller rocks while clutching her neck. A low voice wavering in the wind, whispered, "Take what you find to those who care. They will explain."

Then nothing. Molly was in control again. She immediately scrambled onto the rocks and began to overturn the smaller ones. Breaking her nails and scraping her knuckles, Molly worked furiously.

"This is crazy, I don't even know what I'm looking for!"

The wind gusted up around her as though spurring her on. Using her hands and feet to push the rocks out of the way, she laboured to find something, anything that would satisfy her possessor. Working feverishly to recover the spirit's lost possession, her fear gradually subsided. She began to think of herself less as a victim of an evil spirit and more of an accomplice.

After what seemed like hours of searching, she sank heavily onto a boulder, elbows on her knees and her head in her hands.

"What now?" she said aloud.

The wind offered no help this time. Eyes downcast, Molly kicked a small rock by her foot. Something shiny caught her eye.

"What's that?" she said, reaching down. Wedged between two large rocks was something that sparkled for a moment.

"If I could just . . . get in there . . . a little further!" All of a sudden Molly felt something move. She tugged gently and out came a gold chain with a scratched oval locket.

"This must be it!" she shouted triumphantly.

"We found it!"

Turning the locket over she saw the letters 'AM' engraved on the front.

"I've got to show this to Gran and Grandpa!" Molly yelled into the wind. She scrambled up over the rocks and raced home.

Slamming the screen door behind her, she flew into the kitchen, nearly knocking over her grandfather.

"Look what I found in the rocks!" she cried as she held up the necklace. Her grandparents stared at it astounded.

"Well, what do you think?" Molly gasped.

"I . . . I can't believe it!" said Gran, "You said you found this down in the rocks behind the house?"

Her grandfather held it, turned it over and looked at the initials 'AM'. He shook his head.

"This is amazing, Molly. Your mother, Annie lost this locket when she was just about your age. She was so upset when she lost it, wasn't she, Gert?"

Moving over, he put his arm around Gert's shoulder. "It's simply incredible that you found it after all this time!"

Molly stopped and stared at them.

"Then it must have been my mother who helped me find it," she said confidently.

Her grandparents looked at each other. Molly's grandfather reached over, giving her a reassuring hug.

"We're sure she did, Molly. We're sure she did."

The Trick

Geraldine Hennigar

"What am I doing here?" muttered Brett as he slowly climbed the wide stone steps to The Chester Home for the Aged. If it meant getting into the club and making some friends, he was willing to go through with the trick. Don't be a wimp; get in there, he told himself.

They had all done it, or so they said.

The night before, the Skulls had met at the graveyard. Moose and Bags explained the initiation test. Some test! Moose stood under the oak tree he used as his office.

"All ya have to do," he said, "is find some old guy. Strike up a conversation, see? Then, right in the middle of your nice friendly chat, you jump up and recite the club motto:

We are the Skulls,
We are the Skulls.
Seeking corpses,
Digging graves.
Defying death,
In secret ways.

"Then you run like mad before a nurse catches you," laughed Bags.

"It'll be a great trick!" snickered Moose."Wait till you see the shocked look on his wrinkled face. You'll bust a rib."

Brett agreed. It sounded easy. Now, standing in a room filled with elderly people, he felt differently.

Then Brett saw him. He sat in the far corner of the room, legs covered in a red and white Hudson Bay blanket, rocking his hunched body back and forth. Brett crossed the room, picking his way carefully around the other patients. The old man looked harmless enough. Except for a smooth bald crown, his face and neck were like a wrinkled prune. The long, clawlike fingers of one hand wrapped themselves around an arm of the chair. Brett wondered how the nurses pried them loose at the end of the day. The free hand clutched a gold watch that the old man continually clicked open and snapped shut.

Brett hesitated. Maybe I should forget the whole thing. I could lie. Nope. Somehow the

Skulls would know.

Slowly the old man's eyes began to move. Brett could fell them creep over his body. He wanted desperately to look away but couldn't. At the exact moment their eyes met, the rocking ceased.

This is insane, Brett told himself. The old man motioned the young boy closer. White skin hung from his bony elbow all the way down to an ugly , liver-spotted hand. Like a slow mechanical claw, the arthritic fingers gestured the boy to sit. Brett obeyed. Easing himself into a chair, he now sat directly across from a pair of beady, black eyes. Things were not going as planned.

CLICK!

SNAP!

The watch opened and closed.

"What do you want, kid?" snarled the old man. Brett's thoughts were scrambled. His lips and mouth felt dry.

"Would . . . er . . . would you like me to read to you?" asked Brett, his tongue thick between his teeth.

CLICK!

SNAP!

The sound unravelled Brett's nerves.

"Ha! *YOU*, a mere child, entertain *ME* , The Great Kodaz, the most famous magician who ever lived? Preposterous!"

"You're kidding? You do tricks and stuff?"

"No. Not for years. Progress-- bah! New inventions--rubbish! People lost interest in magic, so I tucked everything away in my trunk."

A pointy finger flicked the watch open.

CLICK!

The old man checked the time with the clock on the nearby mantel. Brett followed his gaze. Nine forty-five. The Skulls met at ten. He had wasted too much time already. Stop thinking and get to it. Come on, don't chicken out now.

A long, ugly thumb squeezed the watch shut.

SNAP!

For the first time, Brett took a good look at the watch. A round metal case lay in the old man's palm. A fine gold chain laced through his fingers. It dangled back and forth, pulling Brett's eyes lower and lower. Soon his eyelids hung like lead weights. He could hear a voice trailing off . . .

"Yes, years ago things were different. People appreciated the fine art of magic. Not like today. These new video computers. Little creatures popping up and eating each other. Nonsense! I tell you, boy, I could make things disappear with the click of my finger . . . ."

Brett closed his eyes, but just for a moment. Got to stay awake. With a full breath, Brett forced his eyes partially open. What he saw drew his eyes wide open.

"Where am I?" gasped Brett. Everyone had

disappeared. He stood alone in a small dimly-lit room. It gave him the feeling of being lost in a deep dark well. The four walls seemed to close in around him. Dampness filled his nostrils and soaked into his clothes. He peered about for a door. None. How strange. Dust particles danced in a single ray of light from an opening high above.

I'm trapped! A tightness swelled in his throat. Wait. Were his eyes playing tricks on him? Something or someone stood opposite the light.

"Who's there?" Brett tried to shout but his voice was barely a whisper. "I said, who's there?" Heartbeats hammered inside his ears. He stepped forward.

"AWWWWW!"

Staring back at Brett was a young boy, hair standing straight up, eyes bulging with terror, face as white as a ghost. He barely had time to recognize his own reflection before turning to run.

"Ouch!" cried Brett as he tripped over a big iron-bound trunk. "Funny I didn't notice it before."

CLICK!

The lock unfastened and the lid slowly rose. Something black flowed over the side. It covered Brett's feet and legs.

"Oh no! Get off, get off! Please--someone

help!" Brett kicked wildly. He brushed at the thing with one hand. It felt velvety soft and slipped easily over his fingers. Cloth? A black cape lay half in, half out of the trunk. Inside sat a black top hat, white kid gloves and a magician's white-tipped wand. Beautiful gold letters ran across the front side of the trunk.

THE GREAT KODAZ

Wow, the old man's stuff! He was telling the truth. Brett thought a moment. It would be fun to try on the costume.

"Come on, have some guts. This is your chance for some fun." Moose's words returned to nag at him. No more wimp-outs, Brett reminded himself. And before he knew it, he stood in front of the mirror dressed as the Great Kodaz. The cape hung limp on the floor and the hat fell to his eyebrows. The white gloves were the only things that fit.

Brett grinned. He had dared himself and taken it. Confident, he was ready. The ray of light was his spotlight , the mirror, his audience.

"Good evening, ladies and gentlemen. Welcome. And now for my first trick . . . . Gee, I can't believe I'm really doing this." Maybe he'd try the ol' rabbit in the hat trick. Hat in one hand, wand in the other, Brett tapped the rim three times. He peered into the mirror imagining an expectant audience staring back. Strange, the hat began to feel heavy. Gee, I'm only messing around. How can . . . . But it wasn't a rabbit that popped over the rim. A two-headed snake twisted its scaly body back and forth, higher and higher, its forked tongues vibrating in and out. Brett's fingers flew open. The hat fell to the floor. The creature slithered towards him. Stepping backward, he raised the wand and accidentally brushed against the cobweb hanging over the full-length mirror. Presto! The cobwebs grew into green vines, leafy arms reaching out for a victim.

"Man-eating plants!" he yelled frantically.

The wand was destructive power in the untrained hand. What evil bit of sorcery did it have planned?

Am I next? As if reading his thoughts, the wand jerked free from the boy's hand. Like an elastic pulled tight then released, it darted around the room out of control.

"No, don't touch me!" screamed Brett as he dodged the horrible thing. Could it rearrange his cells--mold him into something non-living? He felt like an animal of prey, muscles tense, ears alert, eyes searching.

Where did it go? There it was, hanging motionless in mid-air. Weary of the chase it hovered, ready now to move in. Slowly the wand began to turn, gradually building speed until it was a spinning top.

What now? Brett looked puzzled. At that moment the wand fell to the floor and began attacking his sneakers. A whack here, a poke there. It tugged at the laces. He danced about, trying hopelessly to escape the continual beatings. The wand followed him. No, it guided him, closer and closer to the trunk.

"Ouch! Ouch!"

The wand was moving up his legs. It hurt. Brett had never been so frightened in his life. Wait, was the room getting larger?

"No, it's me," gasped Brett. "I'm shrinking." Reaching out he grabbed the lid of the trunk. "This can't be happening." He squeezed the lid as his feet lifted from off the floor.

Creeeek!!

The lid was closing. He would soon have to let go or his fingers would be jammed. No time to waste. He released his grip and prepared to hit the bottom of the trunk. To his surprise, he continued to fall through empty darkness . . . falling . . . falling . . .

SNAP

From high above his head, the trunk locked shut.

" . . . and with a snap of my finger I could make you reappear. Now that's what I call a great trick. Sit straight, boy. Pay attention when people talk to you."

Once again Brett sat across from the old man. He glanced towards the mantel. Nine fifty-five. Have I been asleep for ten minutes? Yes, that must be it. Brett's body was soaked with perspiration. He reached up to wipe his face.

"No . . . how could it . . . ?" gasped Brett. A white glove covered his hand.

The old man smiled.

"Better give that to me, boy. Moose and Bags would never believe you."

A Secret

Scot Jamieson

His eyes were the first thing I noticed changing. They had begun to reflect the firelight . . . like an animal's.

"You were my only friend when I was in first year," Keith was saying, "the only one I could talk to about anything. My buddy Bruce."

"Yeah," I said, looking again at his eyes, "I bet neither of us ever thought we'd still be going to Camp Coweegan after four years. But here we are.   . . . When I think of first year, you know what comes back? Us being bullied by Lawson."

I knew Keith would remember. He'd been Lawson's favourite victim. He shifted uneasily on his log, and threw another branch on the campfire. Then he spoke as if to himself, in a low and bitter voice. "*Why* couldn't that jerk have left me alone? He made me hate him so *much*."

A loon called out from the darkness across the lake and the water around our little island made the occasional quiet sound.

"I don't think there was *anyone* who felt bad about that creep getting drowned."

"Well," said Keith, "everyone *thinks* Lawson drowned, but who can tell, when they never found his body?"

There was that light shining in his eyes again.

"Keith, you know, I never really noticed this with you before, but your eyes are really *glowing* when they catch the firelight."

"Oh," he said, and looked down. "So I better start telling you right now. Remember I said I had a secret to tell you? And you promised you'd keep it to yourself? That's really important, Bruce. You're my best friend and I got to trust you, okay?"

"Okay, sure, Keith," I reassured him. But for some reason I felt I could have used some reassuring myself. I looked around at the tent, pitched over by a cedar thicket, and the canoe, pulled up onto the grass. All was as it should be, although my eyes seemed to particularly notice the strange, jittery shadows cast by the campfire. It was our "overnighter" that all the fourth year campers went on to test our woodsmanship. The

66

next day the big yellow bus would take us back to the city. But tomorrow was starting to seem like a long way off.

"It has to be this particular night that I tell you," said Keith.

"'Cause tomorrow is the last day here?" I asked.

"No. Because there's a full moon tonight."

"A full *moon* ? . . . Hey, you've got a bug on the side of your head, I think."

He reached up and touched it.

"Oh, that's just my ear sticking out," he said, pulling his hair over it.

"Your *ear* ? Are you sure? Let me see," I said, getting up and walking over to him. He just sat there and pulled back his hair a bit, revealing an ear all right, but so freakishly ugly. It was like the ear of a bat, long and pointed, with a few coarse hairs growing out of it. There was a moment of shock, then I realized it must be a fake. I had known Keith for four years at summer camp and I was certain he didn't have ears like that. But when I touched it, my hand jumped back. The ear was hot, feverish. And was certainly real. The flesh had moved under my fingers.

I sat down on the rock beside Keith and put my hand on his forehead. It too was abnormally hot.

"You've got a serious fever," I told him. "Is

that some kind of growth on your ear? Maybe we should try to get back to Coweegan tonight. You should have told me you were so sick. Is that your secret? This is no joke--"

He pushed my hand aside roughly and stood up. He seemed taller than I'd thought he was. "No, it's no joke. Now shut up and listen," he growled, and started pacing aggressively back and forth. I sat still, not knowing what to think. Keith had always been very quiet, maybe too quiet. He had never fought, or fought back. That had fascinated Lawson, although Lawson used to excel at tormenting guys smaller than himself, even if they resisted.

"It started that first year when we were in Cabin D," Keith explained, pacing around the fire. "And Lawson started picking on me. All the time. Every day. He knew I was afraid of him. I was afraid to even tell anyone. But as much as I was scared of Lawson, I was scared more by something else. I didn't know what it was at first. It was like a strange distant sound coming from way inside me. I knew nobody else could hear it, but *I* could hear it. It started getting closer, or louder, the more Lawson bothered me--a horrible sound. It was like a --like a weird howling sound. And Lawson just kept it up, kept it up. He just loved to see me scared, *THE POOR FOOL.*"

A jolt of fear hit me as his voice completely changed on the last three words. The deepest bass I'd ever heard had bounded out of that skinny little body like a beast out of a cage..

"Did you hear that?" he asked suddenly, in his normal voice.

"You mean the way your voice changed?" I croaked faintly.

"No. That sound, that--distant howling."

"Uh, no. I didn't. I don't *think* I did, anyway. Maybe I missed it. I'll keep an ear open for it. Maybe--"

"Okay, okay, Bruce. Just let me do the talking," Keith broke in . He continued his pacing and the story of his secret, only now, every so often, a word or two would be uttered in that ominous bass.

"But in a way, I kind of felt I *made* it through that year. We both figured Lawson wouldn't be back. He'd been in his fourth year and would have been over age. Back in the city, at home, or school, I wasn't hearing *THAT HOWLING* any more. I thought the nightmare was over. When my dad asked me if I wanted to go back to Camp Coweegan again, I started to *LOOK FORRWARD TO IT.* "

He paused and, breathing heavily, began gazing at something behind me. I turned around and saw the full moon rising up from behind the far hills.

"*Any*way," he continued, "you know what happened--Lawson's uncle is part owner of the camp, and got him that job doing dishes in the main kitchen. Lawson was too old to be a camper, all right, but now he was staff. I remember him twisting my arm that first day, asking me, "Sur*prised* to see me, Keithy, eh? Aren't ya? *Aren't* ya?" and every time twisting a little harder. And even then, I wasn't really listening to him. I was hearing . . . something else.

"It kept *GETTING LOUDER* and louder until one night something happened to me. That was the night Lawson--disappeared. I didn't *HEAR IT* after that. Again, I thought the nightmare was over. But when I came back to Coweegan for my third year the next summer, it started again, really loud, right away. And there was another night when--something happened like the night Lawson--drowned."

Neither of us had thought about the fire for a while, and it had died down quite low. I couldn't see Keith too clearly as he paced over on the other side of the fire now, but his breathing seemed to be getting very peculiar, like he was snoring through his nose, almost like snarling. I didn't like the creeping darkness, but something prevented me from getting up and adding wood to the fire.

"That was last year. After camp I was thinking about it, you know, a *lot* , and I got a calendar that showed the cycles of the moon. It was a full moon the night it happened," he breathed.

"*What* happened?" I asked. "What do you mean, '*It* happened'?"

"Okay. Okay," he said, pressing his hands over his ears for a minute, "I don't know if you remember, but there was one night last year I got caught out of the cabin before wake-up and had to clean the outhouses as punishment."

"Yeah, I think I remember you doing the outhouses," I said.

"Well, I was out *early* , all right. I was out *all night*. I couldn't sleep. It was like I was on fire. As soon as I heard the counsellor snore, I snuck out. I started running, *DEEP INTO THE WOODS*. I wasn't scared. Not of anything. The howling got so loud. Then it stopped. And right then I listened and I could hear *every* thing. And the moon--the moon got so *bright*. I could *see* everything. It was like the sun. And then the sun was in my *head*. Rolling around. And I was running, running fast as *A WOLF. A WOLF THAT COULD KILL* anything. You see? I was *it*! I was *power*," he told me, as he kneeled down on one knee and bent over like he was in pain. His body heaved with great snarling gasps.

"Well, um, that's a really interesting experience, buddy. I'm glad you told me about it," I babbled on. "If you want my advice, I could give it you. Uh, *to* you. I will, that is. I will give-you-it. Just see a doctor, eh? That's simple, eh? You must *have* something. Penicillin--"

"No, it's not so simple, " he panted, with his head still down. "After coming to the conclusion about the full moon, I looked up the other two years. To get to the point, it was a full moon the night Lawson got killed. You understand why it's got to be a secret, now? *MAYBE I KILLED HIM!*"

"No, Keith, no," I stammered. "There was no way you could have done anything-to *Lawson*? Hey, the guy was so big. Mr. Lean and Mean. Have you been worrying yourself about this so long for noth--"

His head came up slowly, and then he grinned. A big, *big*, wide grin. As I looked at the teeth, my throat suddenly got so tight, I wondered if I could still breathe. I felt like a plucked chicken.

"*OBVIOUSLY* , on a full moon, I *could* have done something to Lawson," Keith said, turning his head aside. "Remember, I got Davies and Smiley to trade us for their overnighter? It was supposed to be *their* night tonight. But I knew it was going to be a full moon, and *I WANTED YOU TO BE WITH ME* so I could know if it was just my imagination. By the look on your face, I know it isn't."

"Okay," I said, standing up on shaky legs, "so--a secret. But what's going to happen--uh, to--me? Am I guh going tuh to disappear--like Lawson?"

"No!" said Keith, taking off his T-shirt and

revealing a thickly muscled torso, crawling with quickly intercrossing hairs. "I hated Lawson, but you're my friend. Really. My best friend. That's why I wanted to camp on this *island*. So you can take the canoe and get away. *YOURR LIFE IS IN MY HANDS* , but really, mine is in yours. It's even. If you tell, they'll put *A SILVER BULLET IN ME* , or lock me up in a nuthouse and do experiments on me *MY WHOLE LIFE LONG. IT'S SERIOUS!* "

A tear rolled down the grotesque cheek. For an instant, I felt unexpectedly sorry for him. At least *I* could leave the island tonight. I could leave this horror movie--he had to stay.

If it was true what Keith said though, after this one night he'd be all right. He'd have to just be careful never to come back anywhere near Camp Coweegan on a full moon. And for me, it would just be one miserable freezing night floating around on the lake. And having to keep a deadly secret a long, long time.

There was one little problem with Keith's plan though, I thought, as my eyes wandered over towards the canoe. The werewolf part of him had been taking over the Keith part of him more and more as we'd been talking. At exactly what point would the Keith part be gone, and I'd be sitting here talking with a --?

Suddenly I realized how dark it was. The fire had gone out, leaving only a few burning coals. And over there were two other burning coals, coals that could see. His strange eyes were really on fire now. What had Keith said? "--the moon got so *bright*. I could *see* everything. It was like the sun--" . . . And those two coals were now slowly rising up from where Keith had been kneeling, up and up, until they looked way down on me. They must have been seven feet high.

"So I just take the canoe," I whispered, "and come back in the morning?"

"YEAH. BUT YOU BETTER GO NOW ."

I started backing up towards the overturned canoe, forcing my wobbly legs to move. One step. Another. Another. Another.

"*AND BRUCE* ?" the voice came out of the night.

"Yeah?"

"YOU BETTER RRUNN!"

Oh, I ran all right. I scraped most of the paint off the side of the canoe, pushing it right across the rocks and I scraped most of the skin off my leg, probably on the same rocks. And the canoe had a broken crosspiece and I had a big bruise on my arm where I'd landed *on* the crosspiece after hitting the water. I don't remember if my paddling was a classic J-stroke, but I probably set a Camp Coweegan speed record.

A good hundred metres from shore, I slowed down and looked back. I could see the

massive blackness of the island rising above the dense white mist now skimming the lake's surface.

And then I heard the sound of splashing coming out of the swirling mist.

Or was it just my imagination? I listened and listened, not daring to breathe. But I never heard anything more.

A counsellor found his body floating down near the camp the next day. Keith never *was* a very strong swimmer. I told everyone I had no idea why he'd decided to go swimming alone that night. As they say, some things are better kept secret.

Dark Vision

Susan Kirby-Smith

Jonathan bolted upright in bed, eyes wide open.

What was it? he asked himself. A dream? But I wasn't sleeping, I know I wasn't. Yet it had seemed dreamlike, as if in slow motion.

Across the room his identical twin, Stevie, was engrossed in his video game. Both boys had blond hair, bright blue eyes and freckles scattered across their noses. But there the similarity ended. Jonathan was quiet and pensive, whereas Stevie was always in motion.

"Hey Stevie!"

"Mm? Be quiet, I'm on the seventh level. Two more aliens and I'll have set a new record."

"But listen up --"

"Would you BUZZ OFF . . .Oh no! That's it. I'm zapped. Thanks a million, pest. What d'ya want anyhow?"

"Was I asleep just now?"

Stevie pondered for a minute.

"No. You yelled, so I looked up. You were staring at the ceiling like a zombie or something. Why?"

"Nothing . . . it's just that, well, I guess I must've dozed off and had a bad dream." Jonathan sank back into his pillow.

Satisfied, Stevie turned back to attempt another record.

Jonathan stared straight ahead, trying to make sense of what he had just seen . . . .

The railway track through the woods behind his school . . . It was misty; he couldn't see well. His brother, walking alone along the tracks, wearing his old red windbreaker. And then . . . a strangely solid cloud of black fog appearing from behind Stevie. It came from the woods, slithered out. Shapeless, but seeming to be . . . alive? It was surrounding Stevie! Enfolding him! Stevie was struggling, yelling, trying to escape, but he couldn't . . . couldn't escape the darkness.

Jonathan shuddered. It hadn't been a dream, he was sure now. It was a . . . what? Vision? Whatever, he was scared. Something was going to happen to Stevie.

The next day started with the usual frantic rush. Stevie looking for a lost sock, lost homework, fretting over the blond hair that just wouldn't lie flat. Jonathan watched with an amused smile while gathering up his own belongings, and sauntered down to breakfast. He'd almost finished by the time Stevie came tearing downstairs, books flying one way and gym shorts the other. Gulping down a glasss of juice, Stevie was halfway out of the kitchen before Mom collared him and dragged him back.

"Hold it! It's bad enough skipping breakfast, without going out half dressed. Put your windbreaker on, it's damp and foggy."

"Leggo!" Stevie squirmed as he reached inside the closet. "I gotta run -- promised Paul I'd meet him at ten after. Bye!" And he was gone.

"Phew! I get tired just watching him." Mom smiled at Jonathan.

"Mom? I had this really weird . . . uh . . . dream last night. But not like a dream . . . different."

"Mm? What?" She hurried around the kitchen, unplugging the toaster and putting the milk back in the fridge. "A dream? You can tell me all about it at suppertime. I have to dash or I'll be late for work." She picked up her briefcase as they both left the house, and pecked him on the cheek. "Bye honey, see you later!"

Jonathan, lost in thought, was halfway down the block before he realised he'd forgotten his windbreaker. He dashed back to the house, unlocked the front door, and reached into the hall closet. Drat! That Stevie had taken the wrong jacket. He grabbed his brother's red windbreaker and tore off to school, muttering at his scatterbrained brother all the way.

A mile away in the woods behind the school, a murky pool of darkness lay beneath a dying fir tree. For months this ancient being had lain there, dormant. It had spent years maturing in the gloom of its underground cave as part of an immense dark mass. Finally the urge had come to break away, to seek more food, to grow. Pulsing silently, it had left the cave and slunk through the woods, over fields, devouring whatever creature it encountered. But the small woodland animals had not satisfied its hunger. Now, slowly, the darkness began to stir. No more rest. It was time to move on, time to look for . . . nourishment.

"Jonathan? Jonathan!"

Startled, Jonathan looked up to find his history teacher glaring at him.

"It's not like you to daydream, Jonathan. Whatever is the matter with you today?"

"Oh . . . sorry Mrs. Miller . . . I just ---"

"Never mind. Just start work on your quiz or you'll never be finished."

Jonathan picked up his pencil and set to work. But it was no use. He couldn't concentrate. The vision kept intruding. He saw Stevie struggling . . .

The bell rang for recess. Jonathan sighed. His paper was blank, but he handed it in anyway. He'd just have to face the music later.

He wandered along the corridor, deep in thought. What was that thing he'd seen anyhow? It had seemed like a fog, yet strong, alive. It had been pulling Stevie down . . .

CRASH. His books hit the floor and he was surprised to see Tommy Morgan's angry face almost touching his.

"Why don't you look where you're going, you nut? You walked right into me. What's wrong with you anyhow?"

But Jonathan kept his fears to himself and laboured through the day, forgetting books, staring into space, ignoring his friends. His anxiety felt like a claw tearing at his insides.

The school day over, Jonathan hurried across the schoolyard, searching for Stevie amongst the throng of children heading home. There he was. Rounding the corner of the building, Jonathan suddenly stopped, groaning inwardly. Stevie was heading for the shortcut that

trailed through the woods and along the track. Now he'd have to tell Stevie about the dream. His brother would think he was nuts and would laugh at him. But he couldn't ignore this nagging feeling. Angrily, he kicked at the gravel. He would have to follow his brother. He pulled the windbreaker over his head and plunged into the gloom of the woods.

The darkness swirled around the hollow. Where to go? What to do now? It writhed as its need for food increased. Animals, plants, insects - all withered and died as the life was sucked out of them. A sudden rustling broke the silence. The darkness watched, pulsing silently as a fox leapt

through the bushes and pounced. A mouse struggled frantically in its teeth, and then was still. A small pool of red stained the wet grass. Now the darkness moved. The fox was intent upon its meal, but as the darkness moved closer, the animal froze. The hairs on its back rose and a low snarl emerged from its throat. As a damp chill hit the fox, he instinctively backed away, whimpering. The darkness swooped upon the mouse. A few seconds later there was nothing left but a tiny mass of soft grey fur. The pool of red was gone. But the hunger was not. The darkness remembered the two boys. They almost always came this way. It had noticed the red, and red meant nourishment. It hovered momentarily *above the damp earth, and then slowly, silently, writhed toward the tracks.*

"Stevie!" Jonathan yelled at the top of his lungs; but the fog muffled his voice and Stevie trudged on. Jonathan's heart banged wildly against his ribs. That, and the gravel beneath his feet, were the only sounds he could hear.

He came to an abrupt halt and listened carefully. He heard nothing, but felt like something was watching him. What was it? Something wasn't right.

"It's near me!" Jonathan whispered in horror. He spun around, but saw nothing. Taking a deep breath, he turned back and continued to walk, faster now, and then broke into a jog. He could feel it, the damp chill, getting closer, moving around him.

Me? Jonathan's mind spun. But it was Stevie! I saw him in the dream. It was supposed to be--Red! The realisation suddenly hit him--I'm wearing red.

He stoppped as he felt another rush of frigid air. Flesh tingling, he turned around and opened his mouth in a silent scream as the darkness engulfed him in one swift motion.

Stevie could never say what it was that made him turn around, but he did, and what he saw made him freeze in his tracks.

He saw his brother struggling, fighting inside a cloud of darkness. It was all around him, and as Stevie watched it seemed to grow even denser. It seemed almost fluid and always in motion. Jonathan was yelling and fighting to free himself, yet Stevie could hear nothing. Gathering his wits, he tore back along the tracks. As he approached he wiggling mass he hesitated as he felt the wave of cold. If he went in there, would he be caught too? But he had no choice. As he saw his brother sink to his knees, he stepped forward and reached inside.

Wrapped by the icy fog, Jonathan was chilled to the bone. I'm fading, he thought, his breath coming in short gasps as the darkness invaded his mouth. A heavy, mildewed smell surrounded him, making him think of dark mouldy cellars. He began to shiver uncontrollably. Teeth chattering, he fell forward. The darkness felt heavy now, pressing down on his back and shoulders.

The jacket, he thought, if I could just . . . Peering through the gloom, he could barely make out the dim shape of his brother. He gathered his last ounce of strength. "The jacket," he gasped, "get it away . . . ."

Outside the mass of darkness, Stevie was panicking. His hand, numb with cold, groped frantically for his brother, but he could feel nothing. Suddenly, he caught a glimpse of Jonathan's face. He was saying something. Jacket? Something about the jacket! He didn't understand but had no time to think. Using both hands he plunged forward, held on to the windbreaker and pulled. There was a loud tearing sound and he felt the jacket coming over Jonathan's head. He had it! Now what? He stood still just long enough for the darkness to move. With a *whoosh* it left Jonathan and swept toward Stevie. The boy wasted no time. He flung the jacket with all his might along the tracks. The darkness lunged after it. Stevie watched in horror as it swooped upon the red windbreaker. Suddenly, a distant rumbling invaded his dazed mind, and the tracks shuddered beneath his feet.

"A train! Quick, come on!" he hoisted Jonathan, still weak-kneed, to his feet. "MOVE! Let's go!" He heaved again and they rolled together down the embankment. The gravel scattered as the boys tumbled over each other, a tangle of arms and legs. With a tremendous roar the train thundered past. A rush of air flattened their clothes and hair. THUD. The breath was knocked out of them as they hit a tree and came to a sudden stop. Dazed, Stevie watched as the train bore down upon the darkness. The being was devouring the jacket. The boy held his breath.The train tore through the cloud. Black moisture flew in every direction. Stevie breathed out as the train faded into the distance.

"Jonathan? You hear me? Jonathan!" He wrapped his brother's arm around his shoulders, but recoiled as he felt Jonathan's skin. His brother was covered in slime. Black moisture clung to his hair and flattened it against his forehead. His clothing smelled musty and mildewed. Stevie wrinkled his nose . . . .

"Let's go home, c'mon, you're gonna be O.K. It's gone Jonathan."

They stumbled together down the tracks, past the pools of blackness, past the shrivelled jacket.

Still groggy, Jonathan turned to look one last time before heading for warmth and safety. Nothing moved. It was gone.

As the boys faded into the distance, a small pool of darkness beside the track slowly stirred. Within it, a steady pulsing began. It slid into the woods, weakened but alive. It watched as the boys disappeared into the fog. Its prey had escaped - this time. And as the throbbing inside it strengthened, a thousand smaller pools began a pulsing of their own . . . .

The Creature

Norene Smiley

Gilly peered into the clouded mirror above the kitchen sink.

Maybe I should just cut it all off, she thought in dismay. I've tried everything and it just won't lie down. French braids, hair clips; it's still coming out. Rust-coloured tendrils sprang out wildly like cork screws, framing her small pointed face in a frizzy defiant bush.

"Don't hunch, Gilly dear," chirped Aunt Ruth, bustling into the room. "You look like a big brown turnip." Gilly felt those piercing eyes inspecting her. "My, what a tall girl you are for eleven. And that hair!"

Gilly pushed her glasses further up on her nose and wished for the hundredth time that she had gone with her father.

wwwwhhhiiiIIIIEEEEEE! Aunt Ruth rushed to take the kettle off the woodburning stove before the water bubbled over.

"Perhaps your dad will call tonight. Now, wouldn't that be nice."

"Don't think he will, Aunt Ruth. He said it'd be about two weeks before we'd hear from him."

"Well, never you mind. Maybe you'd like to come to the beauty salon with me tomorrow? I always get my hair done on Fridays. I'm sure Betty can fit you in."

Gilly cringed. "Um . . . Aunt Ruth, could I take Jude for a walk to the beach?"

"Why, she certainly would like that. The storm was so bad yesterday, she hardly got out at all."

Gilly grabbed the leash from its hook. "Come on, Jude." The Yarmouth Toller raced to the back door, nails scratching wildly on the tiled floor.

"Don't be too long now, Gillian, you hear? It'll be dark soon." But the screen door had already slammed.

Gilly took a deep breath of the cool evening air. Calling the dog, she ran quickly down the road to the highway. They dashed across and picked their way over the railway tracks and through piles of driftwood to the beach. Here Gilly stopped in dismay.

"Wow! What a mess! Just look at this place."

It was grotesque. Nothing was the same. Grisly tree roots, shards of glass, hunks of plastic and twisted metal lay everywhere. Even the boulders had been rearranged. Everthing was coated in a thick, slimey mud, as if the ocean bottom had been heaved up.

What's this ugly thing, Gilly wondered. She reached down and picked up a shell. She had never seen anything like it before. It was dark green, almost black, with so many wrinkles it looked deformed. Maybe Dad will know what it is, she thought, tucking it into her pocket. He's always going on about mysteries of the deep.

Jude bounded up with a large stick in her mouth, her golden-red coat brown in the fading light.

"Found a treasure, did you? Want to play? Okay, okay girl. Steady." Gilly took the stick and threw it overhand into the calm water where it fell with a splash. Jude stared intently, waiting.

"Fetch!"

The retriever sprang forward and plunged into the Atlantic, heading directly for her target.

Gilly sat on a log and watched the Toller, her thoughts drifting outward like the ever-widening circles in the water. The death of her mother . . . travelling with her father...London, Aberdeen, Rio . . . wherever Oceaneering Inc. sent him. Where was he now? Probably in a saturation chamber fathoms under the ocean. "Big Red" Foster was always called in emergencies to supervise diving and salvage. Their plans to tour Nova Scotia for the month of August had been abruptly changed when her father had received the call from Head Office. "I'm really sorry, honey. We'll make that trip as soon as I get back. Visit with your aunt. Get to know your relatives."

So here she was, stuck on the outskirts of Halifax with Aunt Ruth. I feel like a laboratory specimen. She looks at me like I'm weird or something. And if I have to sit through one more bridge party, I'm gonna throw up all over the silver tea service! Some vacation.

Lost in thought, Gilly failed to notice Jude. The dog slunk up, tail between her legs. The fur on the back of her neck stood straight up, framing her head like a lion's mane. A growl erupted into two sharp barks and Jude backed up until she was pressed against Gilly's knees.

"What's the matter with you! Get lost. You're disgusting. You've got me all covered in muck." Gilly stood up to wipe the slime from her legs. "Yuck, does this stuff stink!"

It was then that she noticed the fog. It crept inland from the basin, swallowing familiar landmarks. This place seems different at night, she thought uneasily. The driftwood looked bizarre and menacing in the darkness. She glanced anxiously over her shoulder at the stand of ancient beech trees, shrouded in the gloom. She felt isolated, alone in the fog.

Suddenly, two black shapes darted across the water in front of her. Gilly gasped, eyes wide in the darkness, heart pounding. Jude barked and gave chase, but they vanished from sight, wings beating rapidly.

"Black ducks! Boy, they sure gave me a scare." Her voice sounded hollow and too loud to her ears. "We should be getting back, old girl. One more fetch before we go?" Gilly threw the stick as far as she could.

"Fetch!"

Jude hesitated, the whites of her eyes showing clearly in the night. "What's the matter with you? Go on now." Gilly gave her a little push. Jude yelped and lunged into the water.

Gilly squinted into the fog. She noticed an odd greenish cast to the basin. That's funny, I don't remember it being that colour before, she thought. A tingle of fear crept up her spine. Something's wrong here, something's terribly wrong. A low ominous drone welled up from the depths, reverberating like a thousand muffled drums. Gilly looked around quickly. A wave of nausea rolled over her, as the stench of decaying seaweed became overpowering. She felt a desperate urge to run.

"*COME ON JUDE* !"

Then Gilly saw it. Something behind the dog.

"*JUDE* ! *SWIM* !" screamed Gilly.

A huge mass rose and ploughed towards her. The dog was lifted on a wall of foaming, churning water and flung onto the shore. Gilly jumped back in panic and fell with a bone-jarring thud over a log. Eyes closed, she heard a crackling roar. Torrents of water poured down, pounding her like a sledge hammer.

"*D-A-D-D-EEEE* !"

And then . . . everthing was still.

It was a moment before Gilly dared to breathe. She felt like she had been hit by a truck. Tasting salt water on her lips, Gilly's mind reeled. Can I move . . . what was . . . ? Something furry crawled up beside her and in a daze she reached out to clutch the quivering dog. Slowly she opened her eyes.

It lay three meters away. Gilly could tell by the way the waves ebbed and flowed that a monstrous body was submerged at the water's edge. A gigantic, serpentine neck stretched onto the beach, grey-white, like a plant hidden from the sun. Its head was massive, larger than Aunt Ruth's Austin. Nothing moved. Gilly wondered if it was dead. Then she noticed a pulsing through the translucent skin. Webbed flaps on the sides of its head began to whir like an insect. A mighty jaw opened and closed, revealing rows of razor-sharp teeth and a blood red tongue that rolled and hissed. Gilly shuddered; her stomach churned.

FIZZ! CRACK! Gilly flinched as tentacles snaked out, showers of sparks sizzling into the night. Acrid fumes, like ammonia, rose up to burn her nostrils. She choked, tears streaming down her cheeks.

To Gilly's horror, the droning began again. Low vibrations intensified until she shook uncontrollably. They soared to an ear-piercing whistle. Then the beach seemed to disintegrate before her eyes. Gilly cowered behind a log as rocks exploded, hurtling sand and stones in all directions. Branches split and fell crashing to earth. She clasped her hands over her ears, a mute wail distorting her face.

The creature raised its head. Two white orbs flashed open. The blinding wave of light hit Gilly, throwing her backwards. Jolted by an intense current of energy, her arms and legs jerked in violent spasms. A stinging sensation ripped through her body like a knife. Help me! I can't stand it! I'm on fire! Gilly's mind screamed. Her eyes felt like burning holes; her skin shrinking, squeezing her tighter, tighter... The last thing she heard was a sucking, scraping sound, and then nothing.

Gilly became aware of Jude whining and licking her face. She shook her head, trying to clear her vision. Everything was blurred. The fog lay on them like a heavy, wet blanket. It covered the deserted beach and almost obscured a deep trough gouged into the sand leading to the water. Gilly slowly got up and staggered in front of the dog who was anxiously herding her up the path. Loose gravel crunched under her sneakers as she scrambled up to the highway. They crossed and began the steep climb to Aunt Ruth's house.

At last they reached the lawn. Gilly hobbled unsteadily up the flagstone walkway. The screen door creaked as she pulled it open and stumbled into the smothering warmth of the kitchen.

"Gillian! I thought you'd never get back. Guess who's here to..." Aunt Ruth's voice trailed off. She groped for the back of a chair with one hand; the other fluttered to her chest. A stunned look of horror spread over her face.

"Where's my little girl?" boomed a deep voice from the hall.

"Dad!" Joy leapt in Gilly like a flame. She reached into her pocket and pulled out the shell, smashed into hundreds of tiny fragments. She started for the hallway but stopped when she caught a movement in the mirror. Slowly she turned towards the reflection, bits of shell slipping through her fingers to the floor.

A small pointed face, pale and scraped, stared back at her through shattered lenses. And surrounding that face was a tangle of hair that had turned completely and utterly white.

Masquerade

Alice Walsh

"Everyone around here has heard about the infamous Captain Bloodsworth," Kip told Adam.

"Kind of a legendary figure," added Jeff, as the trio walked home from school together.

"You're both forgetting that I've only been living here for the past six months," Adam said.

"Well, it's all here," said Kip, holding up the book he had borrowed from the library. "It says that the Dutch captain lived here in Mahone Bay a little more than a hundred years ago. He was captain of the fishing boat *The Devil's Abode* , and had a crew of five men. One Halloween all the crew members disappeared; later their mutilated bodies were found washed ashore. There was also this deaf mute, Rowden, a boy who was about our age. Story has it that he saw Bloodsworth kill the men. To make sure he wouldn't tell anyone what he saw, the captain chopped off Rowden's fingers to the knuckles."

"Is this a true story?" interrupted Adam.

"Well, I don't know for sure, but old Mr. Hennigar who lives down by the shore tells stories about how his grandfather bought bait from Bloodsworth and found fingers mixed in with the scraps of cod and squid."

"Wow, this is really getting creepy," said Adam. "But I still don't understand why you and Jeff want to go to the Patterson's costume party dressed as Captain Bloodsworth and--who was that other guy . . . Rowden?"

"Well, you see, Adam," explained Kip. "Bloodsworth was caught and hanged, but before he died, he cursed the town, saying he would get even. The next Halloween, his ghost was supposed to have returned and killed Rowden."

"Now, on Halloween night, everyone claims to have seen his ghost," laughed Jeff. "He's supposed to have been seen walking along the shore, his white captain's outfit smeared with blood."

"A lot of people around here are so superstitious they're afraid to leave their homes," Kip added.

"It should be a lot of fun," said Jeff. "My uncle works at the Neptune Theatre in Halifax.

He says I can borrow a captain's costume from the props department. I'm even going to be able to use real theatrical makeup."

"It'll be lots of fun," agreed Kip, waving to the figure in the black coat and scarf that was coming towards them. It was Aunt Polly McNeil, as everyone in the bay called her. She was out of breath by the time she reached them; her frail arms didn't look strong enough to hold the large bag of groceries she was carrying.

"Don't do it, lad," she said to Kip; her Scottish accent still thick even after 50 years in Nova Scotia.

"Don't do what?" Kip asked.

"I hear you've been planning to dress up like the dead on Halloween?"

"Well, yeah . . . " Kip stammered. "Jeff is going to the costume party as Captain Bloodsworth and I'm going as Rowden."

"Then 'tis true," she gasped. "You'll be sorry, just you mark my words. 'Tis not good to vex a ghost, lads," she said, waving a black clad finger at them. "Halloween is the time when unsanctified spirits roam the earth. They may become confused."

"We'll try not to confuse them," Jeff told her, trying to keep a straight face.

"Poor Matthew, that was my late husband. God rest his soul." She made the sign of the cross as she spoke. "He had more than one encounter with the ghost of Bloodsworth. One Halloween he tried to attack poor Matthew right out there on the water. Matthew knocked him over with a paddle. Be careful, lads," she said, walking away. "Be sure to drop by the house on Halloween night and I will give you a soul cake."

As soon as the old lady was out of sight, the boys broke into laughter. "Knocked him over with a paddle?" Jeff said, holding on to his stomach.

"What are soul cakes?" Adam wanted to know.

"Little square buns with currants," Kip explained. "She makes them every Halloween. It's a tradition she brought with her from Scotland."

Kip felt an uneasiness in the pit of his stomach. He knew that no one took Aunt Polly seriously. She was overly religious and very superstitious; some even considered her a bit looney. But he couldn't help remembering all the things that Aunt Polly predicted that came true, like the time the boat caught fire in the harbour. And just before Mr. Landry's mother died, wasn't it she who told him there was going to be a death in the family?

He felt bad about laughing at the old lady. He had been fond of her since he was a little boy. He used to go to her house on Halloween looking for soul cakes. He always left with a promise to say extra prayers for her dead relatives. She often told him how blessed he was to have red hair and such lovely freckles. But Kip was almost twelve now and red hair and freckles seemed more like a curse than anything else. He wished he could be more like Jeff, who was a head taller and very blond. As far as the girls at school were concerned, red hair and freckles were not very "macho."

However, as the week wore on, Kip forgot about his red hair, forgot about Aunt Polly and everything else that wasn't connected with the party. He borrowed his grandfather's fishing clothes and had a pair of white gloves dipped in red dye and sewn to look as though the fingers were chopped off.

He would probably have forgotten all about Aunt Polly's warning if he had not run into her on his way to the party. She was coming out of the graveyard, where she always went to pray for her dead relatives on All Hallow's eve. In the light of the high, full moon, Kip saw her face go white at the sight of him. "I wish you wouldn't do it, lad," she told him. "'Tis not too late to turn back." Kip shook his head and shuffled his feet nervously. "Oh, there is going to be trouble, big trouble," she groaned. As she walked away, her lips were set in a straight line and her frail body trembled under her black coat.

Kip watched her until she was out of sight, then turned and ran, his feet flopping back and forth in the large rubber boots. The moon was half hidden now, but cast enough light to make his shadow distorted and grotesque.

By the time he reached the Patterson's, he was out of breath. The single jack-o-lantern on the gate post leered at him as he walked up the gravel path to the house and rang the bell.

As soon as he stepped inside the door, shivers went up his spine. Mrs. Patterson's kitchen, which was usually very cheerful, felt damp and cold. A musky odour hung in the air. The electricity had been turned off and the room was lit by candles that flickered wildly, casting ominous shadows about the room.

Everyone was gathered around the figure in the Captain's costume. Kip sucked in his breath. Two bloodshot eyes stared at him from a pasty gray face. Lips, curled into a snarl, exposed teeth that were yellowed and rotting. There was blood on the shoes and the white pants. As he moved closer, he noticed that there were rope marks resembling bicycle tire tracks on the neck.

"Jeff, it's fantastic! Gee, I don't know how your uncle did it, but you even look taller."

"He hasn't said a word since he got here," Adam told him. "I think he's afraid his makeup will crack or something."

"It's cold in here," someone complained, and Kip noticed that a thick frost was beginning to form on the windows.

"The heat is turned up as high as it will go," Mrs. Patterson apologized. "I'll go make some hot chocolate. That ought to warm everyone."

"No one seems to want to do anything but sit and stare at Jeff," Adam whispered to Kip. "It's like he has a spell over them."

At that moment, Mary Beth, the Patterson's youngest daughter, came into the room. When she saw the figure in the captain's outfit, she dropped her Cabbage Patch doll and went screaming out of the room.

Kip felt knots forming at the pit of his stomach. "Ah, come on, Jeff. Now look what you've done. You frightened Mary Beth." A loud growl came from deep inside the masked figure. Kip jumped back, startled. It was then that he saw the hand; big and hairy with a tattoo of a large snake. The tongue ran the length of his index finger. The serpent's head, which was the size of his whole hand, narrowed at his wrist. The rest of the body curled around his arm, disappearing under the white captain's outfit.

Puzzled, Kip put out his hand. But as his fingers made contact with the other's flesh, a chill went through his whole body. He felt as if his very soul had been touched. He wanted to get up and run, but felt as if he were trapped in a nightmare.

He was still in a daze minutes later when the doorbell rang. "I'll get it," said Mrs. Patterson, setting down a tray of hot chocolate on the kitchen table. She opened the door and gasped.

"Sorry to miss the party, guys," said a voice at the door. "My uncle's car broke down."

All eyes turned quickly to the tall blond boy standing in the doorway in an oversized captain's outfit. Then just as quickly they turned back to stare in terror.

The snarling creature had risen to his feet.